W9-CNB-661

The Unlikely Flying Object

by Susan Docherty

Already available!

ISBN 1-904914-00-4

Sweaterheads.

For Ian, Jennifer, Callum, Ashley, Martin, Mark, Chloe, Terry, Craig, Kristopher, Zack, Hana, Miranda, Calvin, Christina and Echo

Copyright 2004 Susan Docherty
Susan Docherty has asserted her rights under the
Copyright Designs and Patents Act 1988 to be
identified as Author Illustrator of this work
ALL RIGHTS RESERVED

First Edition

Published in Scotland 2004 by
Susan Docherty of Alba Ltd
PO Box 26761
Glasgow
G3 8XQ

Distributed by Sweaterheads Productions Ltd
www.sweaterheads.com

ISBN 1-904914-01-2

A CIP catalogue of this book is
available from the British Library

Printed in Scotland by
J McCormick & Co Ltd
McCormick House, 46 Darnley Street
Glasgow G41 2TY

Layout, cover, photography and design by Sweaterheads Productions Ltd

Lelooni

by Susan Docherty

Lelooni, Intarsia's moon, had just finished his night's work, lighting up Intarsia's sky. He floated down to settle for his day's sleep on the big soft fluffy cloud that was his home and his bed. He wriggled about to get comfortable.

On one side of the sky, Sun was getting hotter. On the other side, Wind puffed from time to time, but not enough to cool Lelooni and let him drift off to sleep. Lelooni was grumpy and restless, hot and cross and very sleepy. Wind just loved to tease Lelooni by blowing him away!

Angrily Lelooni scooped up handfuls of icy cold fluffy cloud and aimed them straight at Sun and Wind. He knocked the wind out of Wind's sails. Next he turned to Sun, aiming a snowball straight at him. Then Lelooni giggled, quite pleased that he'd upset Sun and Wind.

Lelooni could not sleep, so he sat around twiddling his thumbs, looking for mischief to do. He was very bored indeed! Wind had blown away, completely out off puff, and too weak even to blow the pieces of cloud back at Lelooni. Sun was now high in the sky, out of Lelooni's reach. Lelooni tapped his feet, drummed his fingers and rolled his eyes. He then yawned a huge yawn, sighed a long sigh and again tried to sleep. He had nearly dozed off when a hot, searing pain in his leg woke him up.

"Ouch!" he yelped, sitting up sharply. He looked at the sore leg and spotted something pointed sticking in it. Goodness! It was a huge fish hook attached to a fishing line. "Ouch!" he cried again.

Lelooni yanked at the line which dangled from him, again and again until at last WHACK, the whole line and a fishing rod clonked him right on the head!

"Whozzis?" he exclaimed. It was Little Running Stitch's fishing rod, hook, line and sinker!

"Hmmm," muttered Lelooni, "It's a new toy." Pleased at this find, he carefully eased the hook out of his sore leg and started to copy the way he'd once seen Little Running Stitch cast her line. He cast the line up into the sky, not too sure what to expect. The line disappeared below the clouds and moments later he felt a tug. He quickly reeled the line back in. On the end of the hook was a lovely red crocheted cushion.

Far below, Louise gasped in surprise as her brand new red cushion was hooked and whisked out of her bag. Up, up and away into the clouds, it disappeared...

Lelooni cast his line again. This time he hooked a newspaper. It was Pimple's. Pimple had sat down to read the day's news over breakfast in the garden, only to have his paper hooked from his hands. Worse, he had just been reading a bit of juicy gossip!

"Ooh!" gloated Lelooni, grinning. He was pleased with this catch. He giggled at the Intarsian gossip and wept at the sad bits of news. However, when he found an article about himself, he rapidly tired of reading!

"Lies!" he wailed and tossed the paper off his cloud, "All lies." Far below, Pimple was most astonished when his own paper smacked him right on the head and then landed SPLOOSH in his cornflakes!

Lelooni cast his line once more and this time, he hooked a monocle. The Mothership had brought this back from her last trip to Earth along with a lovely hand-held mirror. She was fast asleep on her launch pad, snoring gently and never noticed her loss at all. Lelooni had pinched her prize.

Lelooni played about with the monocle. Curious, he screwed up his face, comically magnifying his own eyes and looking quite hilarious.

Then a little hole appeared in his cloud and he peered down at Planet Intarsia where he spied the hand-mirror, sparkling under Sun's strong glare.

"Wozzat?" he yelled, excited, as his cloud drifted over the Mothership's launch pad. He flapped his arms fiercely to try and move his cloud backwards. Wind spotted this and gave a sneaky puff, blowing Lelooni right off course! Ahh, revenge is sweet. He smirked, and turned the other cheek to puff elsewhere. Wind could not hide his naughty delight.

Frustrated at missing the opportunity to hook the mirror, Lelooni cast his line again. This time, he had his eye on something special. He knew exactly what he wanted. He had spotted Pimple in the distance through his monocle and Pimple had something very interesting. He lowered his hook and line through the cloud and waited while Planet Intarsia spun round just enough. With a quick flick of his wrist he snaffled Pimple's guitar – his most prized possession. Lelooni crowed with delight. "Ooh! What a beautiful gitrrr! Lelooni, Pop Idol", he thought, and his eyes rolled and glazed over as he dreamed of fame! He took out his sunglasses, put them on and started to dance, strumming the guitar and trying to sing. The sound was not at all 'cool'. It was awful!

This time, Pimple saw Lelooni, and was really furious. He ran below the cloud yelling at him in a rage, "Loony-moony, Lelooni!" He shook his fist skywards.

Sun laughed loudly, "Lelooni Tunes!" he shouted, twirling his finger by the side of his head. He gloated wickedly, pleased at how awful Lelooni sounded.

Lelooni was not amused. He tossed the guitar off his cloud and it sped downwards only to smack Pimple right on the nose. Ouch! A flying newspaper had already hit him, and now a flying guitar! Whatever next? "Loony-moony!" he yelled, shaking his fist angrily. But at least he'd got his guitar back and it was fine, even if Pimple wasn't!

Lelooni cast his line again. He was quickly learning that the fishing rod was very useful. He could catch anything he wanted. This time he'd get that hand-mirror. So he waited patiently, peeping through the hole in the cloud to the planet below.

By this time, Intarsia had made another full turn and Lelooni's cloud was hovering above the Mothership's launch pad. With another flick of Lelooni's wrist the hand-mirror had a brand new owner! He reeled in his new trophy, polished it with a handful of soft cloud and peered into it. "Awww, bootiful," he sighed, staring at the handsomest fellow he had ever seen. He gazed into the mirror for a very long time...

Then, out of the corner of his eye, he spotted Sam loading his car with a deckchair and suitcase, for his holiday at the beach. Sam was a well-organised person and had bound the deckchair and suitcase together, so they would stay put when he tied them on the car.

Lelooni gently lowered his fishing line and whipped the neat package up into the air. After untying it he opened up the deckchair and sat down. "Comfy!" he said, smiling.

He opened the suitcase and began exploring the contents. First out was a hat. A hat! Lelooni loved hats. He popped it on his head and pulled out the mirror. "Aww!" He drooled at the image that gazed back at him. He looked so silly. The hat was far too small for him. He didn't care. After all it was a rather nice hat.

Next he rummaged through the case and found a tube of sun cream. Disinterested, Lelooni threw the tube aside and continued his exploration. Then he discovered a pile of ready written postcards. Sam was very organised and had written them all before his holiday! Lelooni held one up to read. 'Having a wonderful time. Lovely weather. Wish you were here.'

"A holiday, mmmmm..." Lelooni's eyes scanned the skies. He looked at Sun, who was having a lunchtime nap, and then he spied a lovely pink and gold-tinged cloud. How inviting and tempting it looked! So, strapping the folded deckchair to his back with Sam's luggage strap, a piece of bright yellow wool, he grabbed the suitcase and got ready to jump onto the puffy cloud as it floated by. With a hop, a skip and a jump Lelooni somersaulted high in the air and landed 'whoof' on top of the pink and gold cloud.

"My very own holiday in the sun," he thought. He unfolded the deckchair, wriggled around to get comfy, then took out his sunglasses and popped them on his big shiny silver nose. His eyelids began to droop. He was very tired after all his adventures.

Lelooni closed his eyes. Sun opened his. He'd been awakened from his nap by Lelooni moving close to him and he didn't like Lelooni's coolness one little bit. Now when Sun got irritated, he got hot, Very hot. In fact he was blazing. Sun shone and shone until Lelooni awoke with a burning heat on his face and limbs. He was throbbing and glowing bright red. Ouch! If only he'd used some of the sun cream that Sam had packed instead of throwing it aside. Silly-Billy-loony-moony!

So instead, he danced about in pain. Lelooni grabbed handfuls of ice-cold cloud and patted his sore face with them. Eventually the coolness soothed his pain and Lelooni, exhausted, sank into a deep sleep, with his arms and legs sticking straight up.

Sun had forgotten his anger as he watched the antics of Lelooni leaping from cloud to cloud in pain. He sniggered out loud, when he saw Lelooni's shiny red face. He looked anything but cool now. Wind was nowhere to be seen, so there was nothing to cool Lelooni down as he slept.

When he woke, Lelooni pulled out the mirror and gazed into it. He shrieked in horror. A strange red face stared back at him. Then it dawned on him that this was himself! He was not happy. Disgusted, he tossed the deckchair and suitcase off the cloud just as he floated above the beach on Intarsia. The unused tube of sun cream speedily followed.

Down below Sam had just parked his little car, and was walking along wishing his holiday would come back. At that very moment his suitcase fell out of the blue sky and plopped right in his path! "Wow," he thought. He picked up the suitcase and walked down the steps towards the beach. Suddenly his deckchair landed right in front of him, all open and ready to sit on. "Thank you," he said to himself. His wish had come true in the strangest way. Sam decided that he'd do a lot more wishing from now on, especially as he seemed to be rather good at it!

As he settled back into his deckchair for a snooze in the sunshine, a small thought sneaked into his head. He decided that he'd save all his future wishes for special, important things. "Can't be too careful what I wish for," he thought. "Never know what I might get!"

Soon he was snoozing happily in the sun, dreaming dreams and snoring soft snores.

Lelooni didn't turn up for work that night. The Loonbeams, whose job it is to light his night light on every shift, were worried and went looking for him. When they found him they realised there was something really wrong with Lelooni. The Loonbeams agreed that something had to be done for him. They disappeared into the night, and returned in a flash with a hospital bed, screen and locker. Lelooni was lifted, still sleeping, into the bed. A thermometer was placed under his tongue. The Loonbeams felt it best to let him rest.

The next morning the Loonbeams came back to see Lelooni. He was now sitting up looking brighter. His old glow was back. All the little Loonbeams danced around him joyfully and he, in turn, juggled with them.

If you've ever touched a Loonbeam, you'll know why Lelooni wanted to juggle with them. They tickle, and Lelooni loved being tickled.

Sun felt ashamed when he saw how ill he'd made Lelooni. So as he passed overhead, he dropped a little package onto the cloud with a card to say sorry. The card had a handsome picture of Sun on the front.

Lelooni squealed with delight as he unwrapped the package. Inside there was a beautiful teddy bear. Lelooni kissed it and snuggled up with it in his cloudy bed. He waved at Sun. He was really pleased with his new teddy.

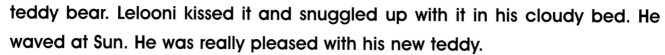

For a few days Lelooni behaved himself, but he soon got bored again. Rummaging about he found the monocle. He peeped through a hole in his cloud. Far below Kate Fit was in her garden working out to the keep-fit music on her radio.

"One, two, three, four,

Reach for the ceiling,

Reach for the floor..."

As Kate bent to touch the ground, Lelooni whisked her radio, earphones and all, up into his cloud. Kate didn't even see it go! She'd been so busy keeping time to the music that she hadn't even noticed it stop! Looking all around her, Kate was ever so puzzled. Where had the radio gone?

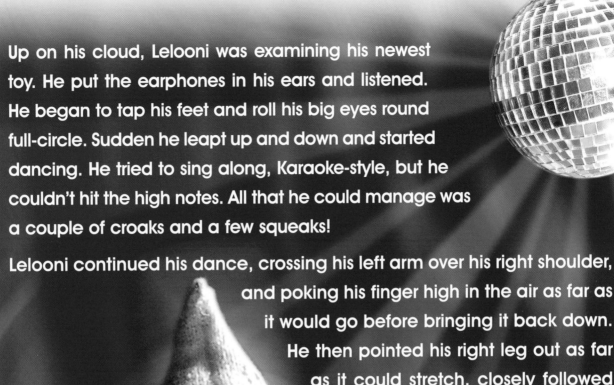

Up on his cloud, Lelooni was examining his newest toy. He put the earphones in his ears and listened. He began to tap his feet and roll his big eyes round full-circle. Sudden he leapt up and down and started dancing. He tried to sing along, Karaoke-style, but he couldn't hit the high notes. All that he could manage was a couple of croaks and a few squeaks!

Lelooni continued his dance, crossing his left arm over his right shoulder, and poking his finger high in the air as far as it would go before bringing it back down. He then pointed his right leg out as far as it could stretch, closely followed by the queerly pointed finger! He repeated this dance several times, but then he stopped very suddenly. There was no music left. It had gone away. Pulling out the earphones he first examined them and then the radio itself. Nothing. In a fit of temper he tossed the radio off the cloud. It landed right back in Kate's garden.

Lelooni brought out the monocle. He eagerly scanned Intarsia for a new toy. But there wasn't anything that caught his eye. Lelooni felt lonely and bored.

Suddenly he jumped over to the very edge of his cloud. Something below had caught his eye. He leapt about his cloud crazily, peeping over the edge. Then he let down his fishing line, all the while peering through the hole in the cloud, ready to pounce. The planet made one full turn before Lelooni spotted what he wanted. He squealed with excitement as it came closer. What could it be? A few moments later it was hooked and he began to pull, heave and strain at the line. He hopped with glee, waving his fists in the air and yelling, "Yes, yes!" At last he pulled his prize catch close and heaved it up onto his cloud. What a weight it was! Lelooni circled his find, looking at it this way and that, clearly puzzled. On the outside, in big gold letters, were the words:

THE GREAT MAGICIAN'S BOX

Lelooni had hooked his prize from a circus lorry passing below on its way to the next town. He opened the box, and squeaked with pleasure at what he saw. First out was a top hat. He put it on at once. He looked a really loony-man-in-the-moony with a teeny-weeny hat perched on the top of his head!

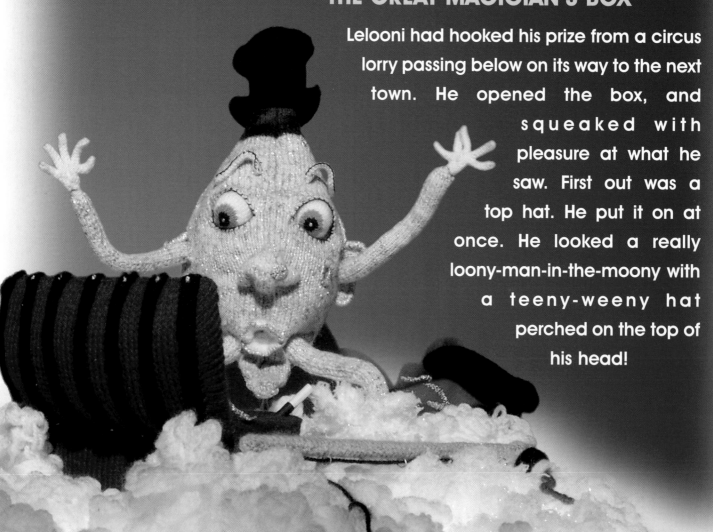

Then Lelooni pulled out a wand.
It was magic! It sparkled and showered puffs
of glittering stardust everywhere. As Lelooni waved it around
a trail of amazing glittering gold stars swept across the sky, but nothing else
seemed to happen. Lots of tiny grey mice had popped out of his hat and
scuttled off, unseen by Lelooni . He kept waving the wand and the
hat's lid lifted again and again. And the mice
with their pink velvety noses, ears
and tails scampered all over
the cloud! They were just
everywhere.

When Lelooni spotted the mice he realised they were coming out of the hat. He whipped it off to see what was going on. He stared into a bottomless black hole! His face was a picture of astonishment. Curious to see where all the mice had come from, he pulled a magic book from the big box. Chapter four, page eight said:

MAGIC TRICKS

Lelooni began to read, 'To make mice appear from the top hat, wave the wand in a full circle,' it said. He put the top hat down in front of him, waved the wand again and, lo and behold, another tiny mouse popped out as if from nowhere! Lelooni looked at the book again. 'To make brightly coloured hankies, wave the wand in an 'M' shape,' the book said. Lelooni waved the wand. He peered into the hat and saw a tiny corner of bright red material. It was a red hanky. Soon there was a huge pile of brightly coloured hankies all over Lelooni's cloud. They looked like bunting at a fair! The mice got excited and started squeaking loudly. Lelooni covered his ears. "I wish that awful noise would stop!" he wailed. As soon as he said that, two hankies jumped up and plugged his ears.

The mice untied the hankies to separate them. They looked just like tiny mouse-blankets and it was mouse bedtime! Soon they all found a comfy little corner and settled down to sleep under their new bedding. "Zzzzzzzz," they all snored happily.

Lelooni yawned. He then scrabbled about to find his teddy bear, plumped up his cushion and fell fast asleep. But not for long! A loud squeaking woke him suddenly and the chief mouse thrust the magic wand at him. Four smaller mice pointed at a page of the magic book they were holding open. It said: 'How to make cheese'. " Ah," thought Lelooni, "the mice are hungry. Poor little things".

'Wave wand in a 'U' shape,' said the book. Lelooni swept the wand into a perfect 'U'. Abracadabra! A huge cheese appeared. There was enough for everyone and Lelooni made sure he had plenty! After the feast, everyone slept soundly.

When
Lelooni woke up
he had a very sore
tummy. He hopped and danced,
and moaned and groaned, all the while
holding his tummy.

Suddenly, out of the blue, there was a sound like a huge clap of thunder. Oops! Lelooni had let loose a 'stinky'! In seconds all the little mice were in a panic, desperately trying to escape the smell. But it was no use. The cloud wasn't big enough. One poor little mouse fainted clean away!

Then the chief mouse had an idea. He whispered to the others. Two by two, the mice grabbed their blankets, and holding two corners in each paw, they parachuted to the ground. Then they disappeared all over Intarsia.

Lelooni was so sad to see them go that he began to cry. All his new friends had abandoned him and deserted his stinky cloud!

If Lelooni had known that a 'stinky' would escape he would have hopped onto a different cloud, so his friends could all have avoided it. Now he sat all alone with his teddy bear and his own 'stinky'! A single tear rolled slowly down Lelooni's cheek.

Wind was sorry to see Lelooni sad so he blew away the stinky. A breath of clean, fresh air, soon cleared the smell away. But Lelooni was still lonely and he wept quietly as he cuddled Teddy, who was the only one who hadn't minded the stinky! Lelooni sucked his fingers for comfort. He sobbed softly into his fluffy pillow.

When the Loonbeams came to wake Lelooni they found a very unhappy moon indeed! So they began to perform their special happy-making musical routine. They sang softly and made tinkling music. Their voices were sweet and soothing and their song was haunting and comforting.

Lelooni knew that the music meant he could make a wish. He wished very hard for a friend who would live with him on his cloud, even if a stinky did happen now and again! The Loonbeams danced and sang and glowed with happiness. They sang this little song to him:

"We'll give you a wish on a Loonbeam,
On a Loonbeam, not on a star,
You could make a wish on a satellite dish
But a Loonbeam is better by far!"

Feeling happier, Lelooni searched his bed for something to dry his eyes. He found a hanky the mice had left behind. He lifted it up, and what do you think he found?

It was the tiny mouse that had fainted clean away, sleeping soundly!

A friend at last! This one hadn't deserted Lelooni when the stinky escaped.

"He must really love me," he thought. What a happy loony-moony Lelooni was! His dearest wish had come true.

From then on, when Lelooni came home after work, there, waiting eagerly for him, were the tiny mouse and Teddy. They'd all curl up together on Lelooni's soft, fluffy Intarsian cloud.

"When I grow up," thought Lelooni, "I'm going to be a magician. One day I may even perform at the big circus." Lelooni yawned.

At long last sleep came over him. Lelooni closed his eyes, he fell into a deep sleep and began dreaming the sweetest dreams. And what did he dream of?

LELOONI-MOONY, MAGICIAN EXTRAORDINAIRE,
Happy dreams Indeed! But that's another story altogether...